Pavilion Press, Inc.
Philadelphia • New York •

Copyright ©2004 by Pavilion Press, Inc.

of Peter Rabbit by Beatrix Potter

Paperback	1-4145-0641-4
Hardcover	1-4145-0655-4

This book is printed on acid-free paper. Designed for readability,

.Library of Congress Cataloging-in-Publication Data
1. children• 2. Potter, Beatrix
3. Fiction • 4.Fables• 5. Easy Reading

First published in 1904; illustrations by Beatrix Potter

Composition by Pavilion Press, Inc. Philadelphia, PA
www.pavilionpress.com

THE TALE OF PETER RABBIT

by

Beatrix Potter

PAVILION PRESS

ONCE upon a time there
were four little Rabbits,
and their names were --
Flopsy,
Mopsy,
Cotton-tail,
and Peter.

They lived with their Mother
in a sand-bank, underneath the
root of a very big fir tree.

``NOW, my dears," said old
Mrs. Rabbit one morning,
``you may go into the fields
or down the lane, but don't go
into Mr. McGregor's garden:
your Father had an accident
there; he was put in a pie by
Mrs. McGregor."

``NOW run along, and don't get into mischief. I am going out.''

THEN old Mrs. Rabbit took
a basket and her umbrella,
and went through the
wood to the baker's. She
bought a loaf of brown bread
and five currant buns.

FLOPSY, Mopsy, and Cotton-
tail, who were good
little bunnies, went down the
lane to gather blackberries;

BUT Peter, who was very
naughty, ran straight
away to Mr. McGregor's
garden, and squeezed under
the gate!

FIRST he ate some lettuces
and some French beans;
and then he ate some radishes;

AND then, feeling rather
sick, he went to look for
some parsley.

BUT round the end of a cucumber frame, whom should he meet but Mr. McGregor!

MR. McGREGOR was on
his hands and knees
planting out young cabbages,
but he jumped up and ran after
Peter, waving a rake and calling
out, ``Stop thief!''

PETER was most dreadfully
frightened; he rushed all
over the garden, for he had
forgotten the way back to the
gate.

He lost one of his shoes
among the cabbages, and the
other shoe amongst the potatoes.

AFTER losing them, he ran
on four legs and went
faster, so that I think he might
have got away altogether if he
had not unfortunately run into
a gooseberry net, and got
caught by the large buttons on
his jacket. It was a blue jacket
with brass buttons, quite new.

PETER gave himself up for
lost, and shed big tears;
but his sobs were overheard by
some friendly sparrows, who
flew to him in great excitement,
and implored him to
exert himself.

MR. McGREGOR came up with a sieve, which he intended to pop upon the top of Peter; but Peter wriggled out just in time, leaving his jacket behind him.

31

AND rushed into the tool-shed, and jumped into a can. It would have been a beautiful thing to hide in, if it had not had so much water in it.

MR. McGREGOR was
quite sure that Peter
was somewhere in the tool-
shed, perhaps hidden underneath
a flower-pot. He began
to turn them over carefully,
looking under each.

Presently Peter sneezed --
``Kertyschoo!'' Mr. McGregor
was after him in no time,

AND tried to put his foot
upon Peter, who jumped
out of a window, upsetting
three plants. The window was
too small for Mr. McGregor,
and he was tired of running
after Peter. He went back to
his work.

PETER sat down to rest;
he was out of breath and
trembling with fright, and he
had not the least idea which
way to go. Also he was very
damp with sitting in that can.

After a time he began to
wander about, going lippity --
lippity -- not very fast, and
looking all around.

HE found a door in a wall;
but it was locked, and
there was no room for a fat
little rabbit to squeeze
underneath.

An old mouse was running
in and out over the stone doorstep,
carrying peas and beans
to her family in the wood.
Peter asked her the way to the
gate, but she had such a large
pea in her mouth that she could
not answer. She only shook
her head at him. Peter began
to cry.

THEN he tried to find his way straight across the garden, but he became more and more puzzled. Presently, he came to a pond where Mr. McGregor filled his water-cans. A white cat was staring at some gold-fish; she sat very, very still, but now and then the tip of her tail twitched as if it were alive. Peter thought it best to go away without speaking to her; he had heard about cats from his cousin, little Benjamin Bunny.

HE went back towards the
tool-shed, but suddenly,
quite close to him, he heard
the noise of a hoe -- scr-r-ritch,
scratch, scratch, scritch. Peter
scuttered underneath the
bushes. But presently, as
nothing happened, he came
out, and climbed upon a wheelbarrow,
and peeped over. The
first thing he saw was Mr.
McGregor hoeing onions. His
back was turned towards
Peter, and beyond him was
the gate!

PETER got down very
quietly off the wheelbarrow,
and started running
as fast as he could go, along
a straight walk behind some
black-currant bushes.

Mr. McGregor caught sight
of him at the corner, but Peter
did not care. He slipped underneath
the gate, and was safe at
last in the wood outside the
garden.

MR. McGREGOR hung up
the little jacket and the
shoes for a scare-crow to
frighten the blackbirds

PETER never stopped running
or looked behind
him till he got home to the
big fir-tree.

He was so tired that he
flopped down upon the nice
soft sand on the floor of the
rabbit-hole, and shut his eyes.
His mother was busy cooking;
she wondered what he had
done with his clothes. It was
the second little jacket and
pair of shoes that Peter had
lost in a fortnight!

I AM sorry to say that Peter
was not very well during
the evening.

His mother put him to bed,
and made some camomile tea;
and she gave a dose of it to
Peter!

``One table-spoonful to be
taken at bed-time."